A Strict Mother . . .

Marvelous Marvin brought out a colorfully decorated box, and asked Lois to stand on it. Marvin announced he was going to jump over Lois *and* the box.

But just then a voice came from the back of the crowd. "Lois! Lois Waller!"

Mrs. Waller pushed to the front. "Lois, come here this instant," she commanded.

Lois hopped off the box and ran to her mother.

"You're twenty minutes late," Mrs. Waller told Lois. "I was worried sick. "

The crowd watched as Mrs. Waller marched Lois off.

Jessica couldn't imagine anything more embarrassing. "Poor Lois," she said, shaking her head. "I'd hate to have Mrs. Waller as my mom."

Bantam Books in the SWEET VALLEY KIDS series

SWEET VALLEY KIDS

LOIS AND THE SLEEPOVER

**Written by
Molly Mia Stewart**

**Created by
FRANCINE PASCAL**

**Illustrated by
Ying-Hwa Hu**

BANTAM BOOKS
NEW YORK • TORONTO • LONDON • SYDNEY • AUCKLAND

RL 2, 005-008

LOIS AND THE SLEEPOVER
A Bantam Book / August 1994

*Sweet Valley High® and Sweet Valley Kids are
trademarks of Francine Pascal*

Conceived by Francine Pascal

*Produced by Daniel Weiss Associates, Inc.
33 West 17th Street
New York, NY 10011*

Cover art by Susan Tang

ISBN: 0-553-48099-5

Published simultaneously in the United States and Canada

*Bantam Books are published by Bantam Books, a division of Bantam
Doubleday Dell Publishing Group, Inc. Its trademark, consisting of the
words "Bantam Books" and the portrayal of a rooster, is Registered in U.S.
Patent and Trademark Office and in other countries. Marca Registrada.
Bantam Books, 1540 Broadway, New York, New York 10036.*

PRINTED IN THE UNITED STATES OF AMERICA

CWO   0 9 8 7 6 5 4 3 2

To Ethan Arlook

CHAPTER 1

Hot and Sticky

"Come on," Elizabeth Wakefield said. "You can go slower than that."

Elizabeth's twin sister, Jessica, giggled. "No, I can't. If I go any slower my bike will fall over."

Elizabeth and Jessica were having a contest to see who could ride their bike to the park *more slowly*. Usually the twins raced to get to the park first. But it was an extremely hot summer day in Sweet Valley. Jessica and Elizabeth agreed it was too hot to hurry.

The girls didn't *always* agree. That's

because they were different in many ways. Jessica and Elizabeth were identical twins. But just because they looked the same on the outside didn't mean that they were the same on the inside.

Jessica liked dolls and playing Let's Pretend. She enjoyed wearing pretty clothes. Jessica wanted to be a princess or a movie star when she grew up.

Elizabeth loved to read and make up adventure stories. She played soccer for the Sweet Valley Soccer League. Elizabeth wanted to be an astronaut or a writer when she grew up.

Despite their differences, even the twins' best friends sometimes had trouble telling them apart. Elizabeth and Jessica both had blue-green eyes and long blond hair with bangs. When they wore matching outfits, it was almost impossible to tell which twin was which without looking at the name bracelets they always wore.

Being twins was special. Jessica and Elizabeth shared a bedroom and secrets. Even though they liked different things, they knew they would always be best friends.

"I'm going to get there last," Jessica called to Elizabeth as she fought with her wobbly handlebar. But a few minutes later Jessica's front wheel bumped up against the curb in front of the park. "Drat," Jessica mumbled.

Elizabeth's wheel touched the curb a few seconds later. "I win!"

Jessica climbed off her bicycle. "Riding slow is harder than riding fast."

"I know," Elizabeth said.

Jessica blew her bangs off her forehead. "I'm hot." Elizabeth pointed to a big tree inside the park. "Let's go sit in the shade."

"Good idea," Jessica said.

The twins walked slowly toward the tree. When they got there, they found Lois Waller sitting underneath.

"Hello," Lois said with a shy smile.

"Hi," Elizabeth said.

"Hi," Jessica added in a less friendly voice.

The twins plopped down in the shade next to Lois.

Lois was chubby. She wore her hair in pigtails. Lois got teased a lot by the other kids. She used to cry all the time and Jessica still thought of her as a crybaby. Elizabeth thought Lois had grown up a lot in the last few months.

"It's awfully hot," Lois commented.

"Sure is," Elizabeth said. "Too hot to play soccer."

Jessica nodded. "It's too hot to play tag, too."

4

"It's even too hot to go on the swings," Lois said.

"I'm really thirsty," Elizabeth said.

"Me, too," Lois said. "I bet I could drink a gallon of water all by myself."

"That's nothing," Jessica said. "I could empty out an entire swimming pool."

"I could slurp up a lake in one big gulp," Elizabeth said.

The three girls giggled.

"Look, there's Amy," Lois said, pointing across the grass.

"Hey, Amy!" Elizabeth yelled. "Over here!"

Amy Sutton was Elizabeth's best friend after Jessica. She saw Elizabeth waving, waved back, and walked toward the tree. Amy's thin blond hair was pulled up into a ponytail. Pieces of hair were stuck to her sweaty face. She was unwrapping a cherry Popsicle.

"Hi," Amy said. "Do you guys want some of my Popsicle?"

"Yes!" Jessica and Elizabeth shouted together.

Amy held out the popsicle. Elizabeth took a big lick. Jessica took a big bite.

Amy offered the popsicle to Lois.

"No, thanks," Lois said. "My mom doesn't like me to share food with other people."

"Don't worry," Amy said. "I'm not sick or anything."

Lois shook her head. "Mom says red food coloring is bad for you."

"OK," Amy said with a shrug. She sat down. The Popsicle was starting to drip on her hand. Amy slurped it.

"Do you guys want to see *Calicos All Around* this evening?" Amy asked. "It's playing at the theater at the mall. Mom and Dad are taking me, and they said I could invite a few friends."

"Sounds *cool*," Elizabeth said.

"Definitely," Jessica agreed with a happy sigh. "I love to go to the movies in the summertime."

"I know," Amy said. "I can already feel the air-conditioning."

"We'll ask our parents as soon as we get home," Elizabeth promised Amy. "I'll call you before dinnertime."

"Great," Amy said. "I wish I could bring Abby to the movie," she added.

Amy didn't have to tell the other girls who Abby was. They all knew Abby was the bird Amy had found in a tree in her backyard the week before.

Abby was a cockatoo—a kind of parrot. She was white with a fan of yellow feathers on her head. Cockatoos come from Australia and Asia, so the Suttons knew Abby must be someone's pet. Someone's *lost* pet.

Mr. and Mrs. Sutton put an ad in the

newspaper saying they had found Abby. So far nobody had called. Amy was beginning to hope nobody would. She loved Abby.

"Abby wouldn't like *Calicos All Around*," Jessica said.

"Why not?" Amy asked.

"It's about cats," Jessica said.

Lois nodded. "Dozens of cats."

"Hundreds of cats," Elizabeth said. "The movie would probably give Abby a birdie heart attack."

"Maybe it would be a good idea to leave her at home," Amy admitted. She turned to face Lois. "Are you going to come?"

"I'd like to, but I can't," Lois said.

"Why not?" Amy asked. "The movie is rated G."

"I know," Lois said. "I'm going to see it with my mom this weekend. She wants us to go together."

"Your mom can come tonight," Amy

said. "We'll be a big happy group."

Lois wrinkled her nose. "I don't think Mom would want to do that."

"You'd have more fun with us," Jessica said.

"I know," Lois agreed. "But Mom says it's important for us to spend time alone together. She'd never let me go with you."

CHAPTER 2

A Cool Cat

"Your mom won't let you come to a movie with us?" Jessica asked Lois.

Lois shook her head.

"That's unbelievable," Jessica said.

Amy shrugged. "Lois's mom has always been strict."

"But she has gotten real strict this summer," Elizabeth said.

"That's true," Lois said. "But it's just because she loves me."

"My parents love Elizabeth and me," Jessica blurted out. "But they still let us do stuff."

Lois looked down. She didn't say anything.

Jessica bit her lip. She hadn't meant to yell at Lois. She wished she could take it back.

Nobody said anything for a few minutes. Amy slurped down the last of her Popsicle and licked her fingers clean.

"Wasn't *Everyone Owns a Camcorder* cool last night?" Elizabeth said, breaking the silence.

"Yeah!" Amy and Jessica said.

Lois looked up and smiled.

Everyone Owns a Camcorder was the twins' favorite TV show. All of their friends loved it, too. None of the kids would dream of missing the show.

Amy laughed. "I liked the video where the man dressed up like a snowman. When he was standing in his yard, he looked just like the real thing. Then some kids walked by his house and he ran after them. Boy, were they surprised!"

"That was great," Elizabeth said. "But I liked the video the woman took of her cat even better."

"That was definitely the coolest," Jessica agreed.

"Maybe you can teach Snowball and Peekaboo to do that," Amy suggested to Lois. Snowball and Peekaboo were Lois's cats.

"Do what?" Lois asked.

"You remember!" Jessica said. "The cat on the show didn't need to use a litter box. Her owner had taught her to use the toilet. She even flushed!"

"You're kidding me," Lois said. "That's incredible."

"Didn't you see the show?" Amy asked.

Lois looked down at her knees. "No, I missed it."

"How come?" Amy asked. "You're always saying how much you love it. Were you sick or something?"

"No," Lois said. "My mom rented a movie. We were watching it together."

"I love renting movies," Elizabeth said. "What did you see?"

Lois shrugged. "I don't remember the name. It was an old black-and-white movie with people singing and dancing. My mom loves those kinds of movies."

"Sounds boring," Jessica said.

"It wasn't that bad," Lois said. "At least the beginning was OK. I fell asleep after that."

"I'm glad my parents don't make me watch the stuff they like," Amy said. "My mom watches the news channel for hours."

"My mom and dad like to watch cooking shows," Elizabeth said with a giggle.

"Blecch!" Jessica said. "It's a good thing they don't try to make us watch those.

They're boring *and* they make me hungry."

Lois nodded. "You guys are lucky," she whispered. "I wish I didn't have to do everything my mother does."

CHAPTER 3

Double Play

"Hi!" Todd Wilkins yelled. He ran up to where Elizabeth, Jessica, Lois, and Amy were sitting.

Elizabeth was happy to see Todd. She was tired of thinking about Lois and Mrs. Waller.

Todd and Elizabeth were good friends. They played on the Sweet Valley Soccer League together. Todd had dark-brown hair and brown eyes. He was a good athlete.

"Do you guys want to play some softball?" Todd asked.

"I do," Jessica said. "Sitting under this tree is getting boring."

"All *four* of us want to play," Elizabeth added.

Todd made a funny face. "All right," he said slowly.

Elizabeth knew Todd wasn't happy about including Lois. Lois was an awful batter, a worse outfielder, *and* she couldn't pitch. Elizabeth was surprised Todd didn't argue about letting her play.

"Come on," Amy said, jumping up. "Let's go!"

Lois got up slowly.

Todd and the girls started to walk toward the softball field. Lois looked a little nervous.

"Thanks," Elizabeth whispered to Todd. "I didn't think you would want Lois to play."

"Usually I wouldn't," Todd admitted.

"But lots of kids are away on vacation. Hardly anyone is at the park. So we need players. Besides, I'm hoping she'll be on the other team."

Elizabeth laughed and shook her head.

They reached the softball field. Elizabeth knew most of the kids who had gathered there. She saw Winston Egbert, Julie Porter, Kisho Murasaki, Eva Simpson, and Ken Matthews.

Todd and Eva were team captains. They chose up players. The twins were both on Todd's team. So was Lois.

"Can I play outfield?" Lois asked Todd.

Elizabeth knew why Lois wanted that position. It was the easiest—especially if someone good was in the outfield with you. Todd threw Lois a glove. "We don't have enough players to have outfielders. Why don't you try third base? You can

18

run back to get long balls. Or at least you can *try*."

"OK," Lois agreed, but she looked uncertain.

Elizabeth was playing first base. When Todd's team was in the field, she kept an eye on Lois across the diamond. Lois looked nervous. And things were just as bad when Todd's team was at bat. When it was Lois's turn to hit, she went down in three pitches. Lois looked miserable. Elizabeth wished she would relax and have fun.

In the third inning Eva hit the ball right to Elizabeth. Elizabeth caught it and tagged Eva out. Then Elizabeth threw the ball to Lois. Lois tagged Winston out at third base. Double play! Elizabeth ran over to congratulate Lois. The rest of their team gathered around.

"Great play, you guys!" Todd said. "Good going, Lois!"

"That was cool!" Jessica added.

"Thanks," Lois said. She grinned, but then a worried expression crossed her face. "What time is it?"

Elizabeth looked at her watch. "Four forty-eight."

Lois took off Todd's glove. "I have to go."

"Don't go now," Elizabeth said. "You're doing really well."

"You're on a lucky streak," Jessica put in.

"We won't have even teams if you leave," Kisho added.

"I'm sorry," Lois said. "But I have to get home."

"But it's not even dinnertime," Todd said.

"My mother is taking me out to eat at a restaurant," Lois explained. "I have to go home to take a bath and change my clothes."

21

"Let me get this straight," Amy said. "You watched a video with your mom last night, you're going out to dinner with her this evening, and you're going to the movies together this weekend."

"Right," Lois said.

"Only babies spend that much time with their mothers," Jessica muttered.

Elizabeth frowned at Jessica. "What's up with your mom?" she asked Lois.

"Well . . . you see, my grandmother just died," Lois blurted out.

Jessica and Elizabeth exchanged sudden sad looks. Elizabeth thought about her own grandparents. All four of them were alive and Elizabeth liked it that way. She knew she would feel awful if any of her grandparents died.

"That's too bad," Elizabeth said. "You must be sad."

"I'm OK," Lois said. "Grandma was really old and really sick. But my mom is upset. She used to see my grandmother every day. She misses her a lot. That's why she wants to spend lots of time with me."

"I hope your mom feels happier soon," Amy said.

"Me, too," Lois agreed. "I've got to go. See you." Lois ran off toward her house.

"Poor Lois," Jessica said.

"Isn't her father dead, too?" Todd asked.

"Yeah," Elizabeth said. "He died when Lois was four. She has a picture of him in her bedroom."

Jessica shivered. "I wish nobody ever had to die."

"Me, too," Elizabeth agreed.

CHAPTER 4

Sizzling

That night after dinner Elizabeth and Jessica went to see *Calicos All Around* with Amy and her parents. The movie was good, but what the twins really enjoyed was the air-conditioning in the theater. The problem was that when the movie was over and they went outside, it felt hotter than ever.

At home the twins changed into their coolest pajamas. They lay in bed on top of their covers, but they still felt too hot to sleep. Mr. Wakefield suggested that Jessica and Elizabeth take their sleeping bags and pillows down to the den, where there was an air conditioner.

"Hurray!" Elizabeth shouted.

When the twins got downstairs, they found their older brother, Steven, stretched out on the couch reading a comic book. "You guys can't sleep down here," he announced.

"Yes, we can," Jessica said. "Dad told us to."

Steven groaned. "Well, don't make too much noise. I'm trying to read."

The twins rolled their eyes at Steven as they spread their sleeping bags out on the floor.

Jessica lay down and closed her eyes, but she couldn't sleep. "I'm still hot," she complained.

"It's cooler down here," Elizabeth said. "But I'm still hot, too."

"I wish I could sleep in the pool," Steven said.

"You'd drown," Jessica pointed out.

"How about sleeping in the backyard?" Elizabeth suggested. "That would be much cooler."

"Especially if you turned the sprinkler on," Steven said.

Jessica sat up. She had just had an idea. "Hey, Lizzie, let's have a campout! Then all of our friends could sleep outside and we'd all be cool."

"Great idea!" Elizabeth exclaimed. "Who should we invite?"

Jessica thought about that. "It's too bad Lila and Ellen are both away on vacation." Lila Fowler and Ellen Riteman were two of Jessica's best friends.

"Lots of other kids are in town," Elizabeth pointed out. "We can invite Amy and Sandra Ferris and Julie Porter."

"Don't forget Eva," Jessica said.

"Right," Elizabeth said. "That would

make . . . umm, six of us. Mom and Dad will probably let us invite a couple more people."

Jessica shrugged. "I can't think of anyone else."

"I have an idea," Elizabeth said. "Let's invite Lois."

"I don't know," Jessica said slowly.

"Oh, come on, Jess. I know you don't like Lois much," Elizabeth said. "But we had fun playing softball with her at the park today."

"We're not going to be playing softball at the sleepover," Jessica pointed out.

"I know," Elizabeth said. "But don't you feel sorry for Lois? Her grandmother just died. And her mom has been really sad. I bet she'd love to come to our campout."

"Well . . ." Jessica said. She did feel bad for Lois. But she wasn't sure she wanted

her at the party. What if Lois started crying? That would ruin everything.

Elizabeth seemed to guess what Jessica was thinking. "You have to admit that Lois has grown up a lot lately."

Jessica knew that was true. She hadn't seen Lois cry in a long time. Jessica couldn't think of any reason not to invite her to the party. After all, Ellen and Lila weren't coming.

"OK," Jessica finally said. "I guess we can invite Lois."

"I'm touched," Steven said. "Now, will you guys please shut up? I told you I was trying to read."

"We'll ask Mom and Dad at breakfast," Elizabeth whispered to Jessica.

"OK," Jessica whispered back. She closed her eyes and tried to sleep. She still couldn't. But now it was because she was too excited about the campout.

CHAPTER 5

Beach Blanket Bummer

"We just have to call Amy and Lois," Jessica told Elizabeth. "Then we'll be finished."

It was the next morning. At breakfast Mr. and Mrs. Wakefield had told the twins they could have a campout. Jessica and Elizabeth had already called Eva, Sandra, and Julie. All three of them were excited about coming.

"I'll call Amy next," Elizabeth decided. She picked up the phone and dialed her friend's number. Mrs. Sutton answered the phone and put Amy on.

"Hi," Elizabeth said to Amy. "Jessica and I are having a campout on Friday night. Do you want to come?"

"I guess so," Amy said.

Elizabeth laughed. "You don't sound very excited about it."

"I'm sorry," Amy said. "It's just that I'm worried about Abby. I don't think she's eaten anything since the day before yesterday. She isn't playing on her swing *and* she isn't talking. She just stays at the bottom of her cage."

"Maybe she's hot," Elizabeth suggested.

"I don't think that's it," Amy said. "I think she's sick. My dad says I'm probably right."

"Then you should take her to a vet," Elizabeth said.

"We're going to," Amy said. "I'm waiting for my dad to get ready. Hold on. I'll ask

31

my mom if I can come to the campout." Amy put down the phone. While she was gone, Elizabeth told Jessica about Abby.

Jessica frowned. "I hope she's OK."

"Me, too," Elizabeth said.

"Mom says I can come," Amy said when she got back on the phone. "I have to hang up now. My dad is ready to go."

"Amy can come," Elizabeth told Jessica after she had gotten off the phone. "Now we just have to call Lois."

"You call her," Jessica said, wrinkling her nose.

"OK," Elizabeth said. Mrs. Wakefield helped the twins look up the Wallers' phone number in the phone book. Elizabeth dialed. Lois answered.

"That sounds great," Lois said after Elizabeth had told her about the campout. "I'll ask my mom if I can come later."

"Why don't you ask her now?" Elizabeth asked.

"We're on our way to the beach," Lois said. "Hey, do you and Jessica want to come?"

Elizabeth grinned. It was still super hot. The beach was the perfect place to spend the day. But Mr. Wakefield was at his office. And Elizabeth knew her mom had a lot of work to do that day. She wouldn't have time to take Elizabeth and Jessica to the beach.

"Hold on," Elizabeth said. "Do you want to go to the beach with Lois?" she whispered to Jessica.

"The beach?" Jessica asked. "Definitely! I'll go ask Mom."

Jessica ran off. A minute later she came back and announced that Mrs. Wakefield said they could go.

"We'll pick you up in a few minutes," Lois told Elizabeth.

As soon as Elizabeth hung up, the twins ran upstairs to change into their bathing suits. They were excited. Jessica and Elizabeth loved going to the beach—especially when it was ninety-five degrees outside.

In the car the twins' legs stuck to the seat. They were hot and sweaty by the time Mrs. Waller found a parking space at the beach. They climbed out of the car and headed across the sand. The water looked terrific.

Elizabeth kicked off her shoes. "The last one in is a rotten egg," she yelled.

Jessica and Elizabeth started to run toward the waves. "Hold it!" Mrs. Waller hollered.

The twins stopped in their tracks. They turned around to stare at Mrs. Waller. Lois was still standing at her mother's side.

"I don't want you in the water unless I'm with you," Mrs. Waller announced.

"How come?" Jessica asked. "There's a lifeguard on duty."

"Better safe than sorry," Mrs. Waller said.

The twins waited impatiently while Mrs. Waller picked out a spot in the sand, spread out her blanket, put up her beach umbrella, pulled off her skirt, and put on her bathing cap.

"I'm sorry," Lois whispered to the twins.

Elizabeth smiled at her. "Don't worry."

When Mrs. Waller was finally ready to swim, the girls dragged her into the surf. The water felt great.

After everyone had cooled off, Jessica splashed Elizabeth. Elizabeth splashed her back. Then Lois got both of them at the same time. A great splashing battle

35

had begun! But at that moment Mrs. Waller decided it was time for all of them to get out of the water.

"What a bummer," Elizabeth whispered to Jessica.

"Super bummer," Jessica agreed.

Back on the beach Mrs. Waller insisted that all three girls sit under an umbrella with sunscreen on.

Jessica leaned toward Lois. "Did you ask your mother about the campout?"

"Not yet," Lois said. "I don't think now is the right time."

Elizabeth didn't know what Lois meant about the right time. When she and Jessica wanted something, they asked for it as soon as possible. But pretty soon Elizabeth guessed what Lois meant—the beach seemed to make Mrs. Waller nervous.

The girls decided to play Frisbee. On

about the second throw, the Frisbee hit Lois in the face. She was fine, but Mrs. Waller insisted the girls stop playing.

Mrs. Waller wouldn't let them climb on the rocks, because she was afraid they would slip and fall.

And when Jessica and Elizabeth wanted to use the money their mother had given them to buy hot dogs and soft-ice-cream cones, Mrs. Waller wouldn't let Lois have any "of that disgusting junk food." So the twins didn't buy any for themselves. They knew it wasn't nice to eat fun food in front of Lois. They put their money away and ate the healthy raw vegetables, tuna sandwiches, and fruit Mrs. Waller had packed.

Lois could tell the twins were miserable. She kept apologizing.

Elizabeth was doing her best to pretend she wasn't unhappy. But being at the beach and not being allowed to do anything fun was worse than staying home. She was glad when it was time to go. Elizabeth felt terrible for Lois. She just hoped Mrs. Waller would let her come to the campout. Lois deserved some fun.

CHAPTER 6

Lois the Lionhearted

"I can't wait for your campout tomorrow," Julie said to the Jessica and Elizabeth the next day at the park.

"I'm getting excited, too," Jessica said.

"Me, too," Elizabeth said.

"Aren't you excited, Amy?" Julie asked.

Amy was sitting on the swing next to Julie, but she wasn't swinging. She was looking down at the ground and kicking up dust. She didn't answer Julie.

"You *are* still coming, aren't you?" Elizabeth asked Amy.

"I guess so," Amy said.

Julie, Elizabeth, and Jessica exchanged worried looks.

"Is something wrong?" Jessica asked Amy.

Amy nodded without looking up. "Abby is really sick."

"What did the vet say?" Elizabeth asked.

"She says Abby has a bad cold," Amy said. "She gave us some medicine to put in her water."

"A cold?" Julie asked. "That doesn't sound so bad."

"It is for a bird," Amy told her. "The vet said she might die."

"That's terrible," Jessica said.

"But even if Abby does die, you could still get a new bird," Elizabeth said gently.

"No way!" Amy yelled. "Abby *has* to get better."

"But Abby isn't even really your bird," Jessica reminded Amy.

"I don't care," Amy said. "I don't care if someone comes and takes her away tomorrow. I just want her to get better. And—and I hope I get to keep Abby."

"Hi, you guys."

Jessica looked up to see who was talking. It was Lois, and she didn't look much happier than Amy.

"I'm not allowed to come to the camp-out," Lois announced.

"Why not?" Elizabeth asked.

"My mother is having a cookout tomorrow night," Lois explained. "I have to stay home and help."

"What a drag," Jessica said.

"Mom only invited grown-ups," Lois said. "I'm going to be so bored."

"Don't worry," Elizabeth told her. "We'll invite you to our next party."

Lois forced herself to smile. "Maybe my mother won't be acting so strict by then."

Jessica looked from Amy to Lois. She felt as if she were surrounded by unhappy people. But then something wonderful happened.

"Hurry up, you guys," Winston yelled as he ran by the swings. "Marvin the Magnificent is here!"

"All right!" Jessica exclaimed.

Marvin the Magnificent was a street performer. He told jokes and did amazing tricks. Marvin could ride a unicycle. And eat fire!

"Come on," Elizabeth shouted as she jumped up. "Let's go!"

The girls ran after Winston.

A circle of kids had formed around Marvin by the time the twins and their friends joined the crowd. Elizabeth, Jessica, Lois, Amy, and Julie wiggled their way to the front, where they could see everything.

"I'm going to need a volunteer," Marvin

yelled. "But don't raise your hands yet. The volunteer has to be very *brave*."

In a flash Jessica, Elizabeth, Julie, and Amy raised their hands. Lois hesitated, but then she raised hers, too.

Marvin pointed to Lois. "Here's a young lady who looks extremely brave. Come on up."

Lois grinned as she walked into the circle of onlookers. "What's your name?" Marvin asked.

Lois whispered it in his ear.

Marvin held up Lois's arm. "I want you to meet my fearless assistant!" he bellowed. "Lois the Lionhearted!"

And Lois *was* brave. She stood perfectly still while Marvin rode his skateboard right up behind her—and then jumped over her head! Marvin's skateboard zoomed through Lois's legs. He landed on it right in front of her.

Everyone clapped.

"All right, Lois!" Elizabeth yelled. "Way to go."

Marvin brought out a colorfully decorated box. He put the box down with a flourish and asked Lois to stand on it. Marvin announced he was going to jump over Lois *and* the box.

"I can't wait to see this," Julie whispered.

But just then a voice came from the back of the crowd. "Lois! Lois Waller!"

"Oh, no," Amy said. "I know who *that* is."

Mrs. Waller pushed to the front of the crowd. "Lois, come here this instant," she commanded.

Lois hopped off the box and ran to her mother.

The crowd quieted down. They wanted to see what would happen next.

"You're twenty minutes late," Mrs.

Waller told Lois. "I was worried sick. And haven't I told you not to talk to strangers?"

"But Mom, Marvin isn't a stranger," Lois explained. "Everyone knows him."

"Well, *I* don't know him," Mrs. Waller said. "And I don't want you to talk to him anymore."

The crowd watched as Mrs. Waller marched Lois off.

Jessica couldn't imagine anything more embarrassing. "Poor Lois," she said, shaking her head. "I'd hate to have Mrs. Waller as my mom."

CHAPTER 7

Crash! Bang! Boom!

"I can't believe this," Elizabeth groaned as she peered out the kitchen window.

"It's the worst," Jessica said.

It was the night of the twins' campout. Everything was ready for the party. The kitchen was stocked with yummy food. Mr. Wakefield had taken Steven out to dinner and a movie. The only problem was that it was raining *hard*. Every few minutes lightning flashed and thunder boomed.

Elizabeth was holding a bag with Mr.

and Mrs. Wakefield's tent inside. (The twins had their own tent, but it was very small. Mr. and Mrs. Wakefield's tent was big enough for all of the twins' friends.) Jessica and Elizabeth were still hoping it would clear up enough for them to camp out.

Mrs. Wakefield looked out the window. "I'm afraid this isn't going to break until morning," she said with a frown. "Why don't I help you set up the tent in the den?"

Jessica sighed.

Elizabeth felt sad, too. But she knew her mother was right. Sleeping outside in the rain wouldn't be much fun.

"OK," Elizabeth told her mother.

Mrs. Wakefield winked at Elizabeth. "Don't worry. I think you're going to have a great sleepover even if you can't camp out."

"Maybe," Elizabeth said.

A few minutes later, the twins and Mrs. Wakefield had finished putting up the tent. It was fun crawling in and out of it, but Elizabeth couldn't help feeling disappointed.

The doorbell rang.

"Why don't the two of you get that?" Mrs. Wakefield asked. "I bet it's one of your guests."

Jessica and Elizabeth ran into the front hall and threw open the door. It was Amy, and she was grinning.

"Hi," Amy said. "I brought a special guest!" Carefully, Amy took Abby out from under her raincoat. The bird's cage was sitting at Amy's feet.

Elizabeth gasped. "She's beautiful!"

"Is she better?" Jessica asked.

"I'm feeling fine!" Abby squawked.

Amy and the twins laughed. Amy explained that her mother had called Mrs. Wakefield earlier in the afternoon to see if it was all right for her to bring Abby.

Elizabeth and Jessica led Amy and Abby into the den. Amy put Abby's cage down near the tent and Abby hopped inside.

The doorbell rang again. This time it was Sandra and Julie. Sandra was in a great mood. "I love thunderstorms!" she exclaimed. "And this one is really noisy!"

By the time Eva arrived a few minutes later, everyone was having a good time. They were even happier when Mrs. Wakefield brought out a platter of tacos.

"Let's tell ghost stories," Julie suggested when everyone had finished eating. "The storm will make them really spooky."

"Great idea," Jessica said.

"I'll go first," Eva volunteered.

Jessica got a bowl of popcorn. Elizabeth

turned down the lights. The girls sat in a circle in front of the tent.

"One dark and stormy night, a young girl was baby-sitting alone," Eva started. "The house where she was baby-sitting was in the middle of an ancient forest. There wasn't another house around for miles."

Outside, lightning flashed.

"After the baby-sitter put the kids to bed, she tried to read," Eva went on. "But she kept hearing a strange sound coming from outside. Th-rump, th-rump, th-rump. The girl got up and looked out the window. . . ."

Elizabeth felt shivers racing up her back. She glanced toward the den window. A figure was standing outside! Elizabeth covered her mouth with one hand and screamed.

CHAPTER 8

A Mysterious Guest

Jessica spun around to face Elizabeth. "What's wrong?"

"Are you OK?" Sandra asked.

"The story isn't that scary," Eva said.

Elizabeth let out her breath in a huge sigh. "I'm—I'm fine. It's just that Lois scared me." She pointed to the window. "Look, Lois is standing outside."

"I'll go let her in," Jessica said, motioning Lois to the front of the house. She jumped up and ran to the front door. A minute later, Jessica led Lois into the den.

"Hi," Lois said to everyone.

"You're soaking wet!" Sandra exclaimed.

"You scared me half to death," Elizabeth told Lois.

Eva laughed. "And Elizabeth scared the rest of us. She started screaming before I even got to the scary part of my ghost story."

"Why didn't you just ring the doorbell?" Amy asked Lois.

"Umm . . . ," Lois said.

"I bet you *wanted* to scare us," Jessica put in.

"Right!" Lois said. "I wanted to scare you."

"How did you get so wet?" Jessica asked.

"I walked here," Lois explained. "It's pouring."

Jessica frowned when she heard Lois's explanation. It was dark out. She knew Mrs. Waller would never let Lois walk to the Wakefields' by herself at night during a storm. Jessica guessed Lois didn't have permission to be at her house.

"How come you walked?" Jessica asked. "Why didn't your mom drive you?"

"Because she doesn't know I'm here," Lois whispered. Tears welled up in her eyes. "I sneaked out."

"Wow," Jessica said. She was impressed Lois had been brave enough to do that.

The tears started to stream down Lois's face.

Elizabeth put her arm around her. "It's going to be OK. Just tell us what happened."

Lois took a few deep breaths. "Well, when it started to rain, my mother called off her cookout," she said in a quivery voice. "So I asked her if I could come to your party. She said no. She wanted me to stay home with her."

"That was selfish," Sandra said.

Lois nodded. "I was really mad. I told my mom she was being totally unfair. Then I ran up to my room. I couldn't stop thinking about all the fun you guys were having. So I decided to sneak out and come to the party."

"Don't you think your mom will notice you're gone?" Elizabeth asked.

"I'm going to sneak back in before she finds out," Lois said.

"It's probably too late," Sandra said.

"I bet she already noticed," Amy added.

Lois looked horrified. "Do you really think so?"

Eva nodded. "Moms know everything."

The phone rang.

"I bet that's your mom now, Lois!" Amy said.

Lois's eyes got big. "Hide me!"

"Crawl inside the tent," Jessica suggested.

57

Lois crawled in. Julie zipped the flap shut. Just as Julie finished, Mrs. Wakefield came into the den.

"Is Lois here?" Mrs. Wakefield asked. "Mrs. Waller just called and said she's missing."

Elizabeth and Jessica exchanged looks.

Jessica knew Elizabeth would never lie to their mother. "She isn't here," Jessica said quickly.

"Didn't I hear you open the front door?" Mrs. Wakefield asked.

"Yes," Sandra said. "We thought we saw a ghost in the yard. That's why Elizabeth screamed."

Mrs. Wakefield smiled and turned back toward the kitchen. "OK, but try not to scare each other too much."

"Whew," Amy said as soon as Mrs. Wakefield was gone.

"That was close," Abby squawked.

The girls laughed.

"You can come out now," Sandra whispered to Lois.

When Lois got out of the tent, she was crying harder than ever. "I'm going to be in huge trouble."

Jessica didn't blame Lois for crying. She remembered what Mrs. Waller had done in the park—and talking to strangers was nothing compared to sneaking out at night. Mrs. Waller was going to be very angry when she found Lois.

"Don't worry, Lois," Jessica said. "We'll hide you."

CHAPTER 9

Poor Mrs. Waller

Jessica looked thoughtful. "If we're going to hide Lois, we need a plan."

"A plan?" Elizabeth repeated. "What kind of plan?"

"Well, I'll be the guard," Jessica announced. "I'll sit next to the door and watch for Mom. If she comes, I'll start coughing really hard. That'll be the signal."

"That sounds good," Eva said. "Lois, you should sit next to the tent. If Jessica gives the signal, crawl inside. I'll zip up the flap so that no one can see you."

Lois sniffled and nodded. "OK."

The girls took their places. Then Eva told the rest of her ghost story. After Eva finished, Elizabeth went into the kitchen to get more popcorn. She found Mrs. Wakefield staring out the window.

"What's wrong, Mom?" Elizabeth asked.

"I was just wondering where Lois could be," Mrs. Wakefield said. "Poor Mrs. Waller sounded so upset when she called."

"What's Mrs. Waller going to do?" Elizabeth asked.

"I don't know," Mrs. Wakefield said. "She's talking to the police now."

"The police?" Elizabeth repeated. "Wow!"

"Do you know any reason why Lois might have run away?" Mrs. Wakefield asked.

Elizabeth nodded. "Mrs. Waller has been super strict lately," she said. "She wants Lois to spend all of her time with her. Lois is getting really sick of it."

"I see," Mrs. Wakefield said. Then she smiled at Elizabeth. "Don't worry about this too much, honey. Everything will work itself out. Just have a good time with your friends."

"I will, Mom," Elizabeth said. She picked up the popcorn and rushed back into the den. Elizabeth told the others what Mrs. Wakefield had said about the police.

Lois stood up right away. "I have to go. Thanks for the party and hiding me and everything. I'll see you guys later."

"You can't leave. It's pouring cats and dogs out," Jessica said.

"And birds," Abby squawked, hopping out through the open cage door and perching on Amy's shoulder.

Everyone laughed but Lois. "I have to go home," she insisted. "Maybe I can

sneak back in and convince my mom I was there all along."

"Don't do that, Lois," Sandra said.

Julie shook her head. "It's too late for you to be out alone."

"Besides, your mom already knows you're gone," Elizabeth pointed out. "She'll be even angrier if you lie to her."

"Honesty is the best policy," Abby squawked. She pulled on Amy's hair.

"Mind your own business," Lois told the bird.

"But Abby is right," Amy said. "You should turn yourself in."

Lois looked around the circle of faces. One by one the girls nodded their agreement.

Elizabeth took Lois's hand. "Come on. Let's go talk to my mom."

Lois let Elizabeth lead her down the

hallway. Jessica and the other girls followed right behind them.

"Mom," Jessica said quietly as they walked into the kitchen. "We have something to tell you."

Mrs. Wakefield looked up from the newspaper she was reading. "Lois!" she said. "I'm so happy to see you!"

Mrs. Wakefield rushed to the phone and called Mrs. Waller. Lois's mom said she would come right over. The twins and their friends sat down at the kitchen table to wait. Nobody seemed to have anything to say.

Jessica's stomach hurt. She noticed that everyone else looked worried, too. She wondered what would happen when Mrs. Waller arrived.

CHAPTER 10

Guest of Honor

"Lois!" Mrs. Waller yelled as she rushed into the Wakefields' kitchen. "Are you all right?"

As soon as Lois saw her mother, she started to cry again.

"I'm sorry, Mom," Lois choked out. "I didn't mean to run away. I just wanted to come to the party for a little while."

"I'm just happy you're all right," Mrs. Waller told Lois. Her eyes were full of tears. "I thought you might have been hit by a car or gotten lost or—"

"I'm fine," Lois said.

Mrs. Waller gave Lois a long, long bear hug. When she finally let go, she turned to Mrs. Wakefield. "I'm sorry for causing such a fuss. I feel as if I owe you an explanation."

"It's really not—" Mrs. Wakefield started.

But Mrs. Waller held up a hand. "I insist," she said. "See, my mother died a few weeks ago. I guess you know my husband has been dead for years. Lois is the only person I have left now. Tonight I thought I almost lost her, too."

"I understand," Mrs. Wakefield said. "But if I may . . ." Mrs. Wakefield stopped talking and shook her head. "Never mind. It's really none of my business."

"Please go on," Mrs. Waller said.

Jessica nodded at her mom.

Mrs. Wakefield sighed. "Well, it's just that Lois is usually such a good girl.

67

Sneaking out isn't her style. I think that maybe . . . maybe you should give her more freedom. Otherwise you *will* lose her."

Mrs. Waller looked at Lois. "Are you unhappy?" she asked, stroking Lois's hair.

"I love you, Mom," Lois said. "But I can't spend *all* of my time with you. I want to be with my friends, too."

Mrs. Waller didn't say anything for a moment. Then she sighed. "I'm sorry, honey. I was wrong not to let you come tonight," she told Lois. "Would you like to stay?"

"Yes!" Lois yelled.

"All right!" Elizabeth exclaimed.

"Is that OK with you?" Mrs. Waller asked Mrs. Wakefield.

"Of course," Mrs. Wakefield said with a laugh.

"Thank you!" Lois told her mom.

"Thank you," she added to Mrs. Wake-field.

"You're welcome," the grown-ups said together.

"Would you like something to eat or drink?" Mrs. Wakefield asked Mrs. Waller. "I have lots of soft drinks and tacos."

Mrs. Waller sank into a chair. "I'd love some of everything."

Jessica took Lois's hand. "Come on," she said. "We'll find you some pajamas. And you can use Steven's sleeping bag."

"I'm really happy you get to stay," Elizabeth told Lois as the girls trooped up the stairs.

"Me, too," Jessica said. "You can be our guest of honor."

Lois smiled. "That sounds great."

The next morning Jessica woke up in her sleeping bag on the floor of the den.

Elizabeth was already awake. "Shh," she whispered. "Everyone else is still asleep."

"OK," Jessica whispered back.

Jessica crawled out of her sleeping bag, tiptoed around her sleeping friends, and turned on the television low. The twins lay on their sleeping bags and watched TV while they waited for everyone else to get up.

Julie opened her eyes during the next commercial. "What are you watching?"

"A karate cartoon," Jessica said.

Julie sat up. "Really? I love karate."

"You do?" Jessica asked. "How come?"

"It looks like fun," Julie said. "I'm trying to talk my parents into signing me up for lessons."

"I thought only boys could take karate," Sandra said from her spot on the floor.

"No way!" Julie said. "Girls can take karate, too."

Can a girl be good at karate? Find out in Sweet Valley Kids #52, JULIE **THE KARATE KID.**

SIGN UP FOR THE SWEET VALLEY HIGH® FAN CLUB!

Hey, girls! Get all the gossip on Sweet Valley High's® most popular teenagers when you join our fantastic Fan Club! As a member, you'll get all of this really cool stuff:

- Membership Card with your own personal Fan Club ID number
- A Sweet Valley High® Secret Treasure Box
- Sweet Valley High® Stationery
- Official Fan Club Pencil (for secret note writing!)
- Three Bookmarks
- A "Members Only" Door Hanger
- Two Skeins of J. & P. Coats® Embroidery Floss with flower barrette instruction leaflet
- Two editions of *The Oracle* newsletter
- Plus exclusive Sweet Valley High® product offers, special savings, contests, and much more!

Be the first to find out what Jessica & Elizabeth Wakefield are up to by joining the Sweet Valley High® Fan Club for the one-year membership fee of only $6.25 each for U.S. residents, $8.25 for Canadian residents (U.S. currency). Includes shipping & handling.

Send a check or money order (do not send cash) made payable to "Sweet Valley High® Fan Club" along with this form to:

SWEET VALLEY HIGH® FAN CLUB, BOX 3919-B, SCHAUMBURG, IL 60168-3919

NAME_____
(Please print clearly)

ADDRESS_____

CITY_____ STATE _____ ZIP_____
(Required)

AGE_____ BIRTHDAY_____ /_____ /_____